KEVIN HENKES

JULIUS'S CANDY CORN

A Greenwillow Book
HarperFestival®
A Division of HarperCollinsPublishers

Julius was ready for the Halloween party.

Julius's mother had baked cupcakes.

Each cupcake had a candy corn on top.

"Beautiful," said Julius.

"You can't eat the cupcakes yet,"

said Julius's mother.

"They're for the party."

So Julius started counting instead.

"One candy corn," said Julius.

"Another candy corn."

Julius kept counting.

"Another candy corn.

Another candy corn.

Another candy corn."

"All done!" said Julius.

He hadn't eaten the cupcakes.

But he'd counted all the candy corn.

Just then the doorbell rang.

Julius's friends had arrived.

Finally, the party could begin.

"Time for cupcakes!" said Julius.

DELICIOUS !